Dear Parent:
Your child's love of reading starts here!

Every child learns to read in a different way and at his or her own speed. Some go back and forth between reading levels and read favorite books again and again. Others read through each level in order. You can help your young reader improve and become more confident by encouraging his or her own interests and abilities. From books your child reads with you to the first books he or she reads alone, there are I Can Read Books for every stage of reading:

SHARED READING
Basic language, word repetition, and whimsical illustrations, ideal for sharing with your emergent reader

BEGINNING READING
Short sentences, familiar words, and simple concepts for children eager to read on their own

READING WITH HELP
Engaging stories, longer sentences, and language play for developing readers

READING ALONE
Complex plots, challenging vocabulary, and high-interest topics for the independent reader

ADVANCED READING
Short paragraphs, chapters, and exciting themes for the perfect bridge to chapter books

I Can Read Books have introduced children to the joy of reading since 1957. Featuring award-winning authors and illustrators and a fabulous cast of beloved characters, I Can Read Books set the standard for beginning readers.

A lifetime of discovery begins with the magical words "I Can Read!"

Visit www.icanread.com for information
on enriching your child's reading experience.

The Berenstain Bears'
New Kitten

The Berenstain Bears' New Kitten copyright © 2007 by Berenstain Bears, Inc. All rights reserved. No part of this book may be used or reproduced in any manner whatsoever without written permission except in the case of brief quotations embodied in critical articles and reviews. Printed in the United States of America. For information address HarperCollins Children's Books, a division of HarperCollins Publishers, 1350 Avenue of the Americas, New York, NY 10019. www.icanread.com

Library of Congress Cataloging-in-Publication Data

Berenstain, Stan, 1923-

   The Berenstain Bears' new kitten / Stan & Jan Berenstain with Mike Berenstain.—1st ed.

     p. cm.

   Summary: One day while Brother Bear was hunting bullfrogs, he found a tiny, muddy kitten instead, and when he took her home and introduced her to Mama, Papa, Sister, and the family dog, they all decided to keep her.

   ISBN-10: 0-06-058357-6 (pbk.) — ISBN-13: 978-0-06-058357-6 (pbk.)

   ISBN-10: 0-06-058356-8 (trade bdg.) — ISBN-13: 978-0-06-058356-9 (trade bdg.)

    [1. Cats—Fiction. 2. Animals—Infancy—Fiction. 3. Bears—Fiction.] I. Berenstain, Jan, 1923- II. Berenstain, Michael. III. Title.

PZ7.B4483Bfa 2005   2006036335

[E]—dc22   CIP

                                                                              AC

❖

First Edition

I Can Read!

BEGINNING 1 READING

The Berenstain Bears'

New Kitten

Stan & Jan Berenstain
with Mike Berenstain

HarperCollins*Publishers*

One day Brother Bear
was hunting bullfrogs.
He was about to catch a big one.
He heard a tiny *"Mew! Mew!"*
It was a kitten.

The kitten was trying to climb
the muddy bank of the pond.
The kitten was so covered with mud
that you couldn't tell
what color it was.

Someone else was hunting bullfrogs.

"Whatcha got there?" asked Too-Tall from the bushes.

Too-Tall worried Brother.

He was head of a schoolyard gang.

"Never mind what I've got," said Brother.

"Hey!" said Too-Tall.

"A kitten! A poor little shivering kitten."

How about that? thought Brother.

Even Too-Tall has a soft spot

in his heart for kittens.

"You'd better take it home to your mother,"

said Too-Tall.

"Here. Take it home in this!"

With that he gave Brother his hat.

Brother was surprised.

Brother ran home with the kitten
in Too-Tall's hat.

"Hmm," said Mama Bear.

"You go looking for bullfrogs

and you bring home this little kitten."

"May we keep it, Mama?" asked Sister Bear.

"May we please?"

"Never mind about that," said Mama.

"This kitten needs cleaning up."

She turned to

Papa Bear for help.

"Papa," she said, "we need
some warm water,
some cotton balls,
and washrags."

Mama went to work.

She washed the mud off.

She cleaned the
kitten's eyes.

She cleaned its
paws.

Pretty soon it began
to look like a kitten,
not a muddy ball of
fur.

17

Little Lady, the family's dog,

came sniffing around.

"Papa," said Mama,

"would you please take Little Lady?"

"Yes, my dear," said Papa.

"I think the kitten needs a name."

He took a quick look at the kitten's bottom.

"She's a she," he said.

"So I guess we'd better
give her a girl's name."

That made the cubs' ears perk up.
You don't name a kitten
if you're not going to keep her.
"Well," said Sister, "she's gray."

Now that she was clean and dried
and combed, she was a beautiful gray.
Gray, thought Sister.
"Let's name her Gracie!"

"Fine with me," said Mama.

"Now about keeping her.

Have you forgotten that we have a dog?

Though she's a kitten now,

she'll soon be a cat.

Dogs and cats don't always get along."

"Your mama's right," said Papa.
"Let's introduce them right now
and find out."

Little Lady was underfoot again,

sniffing around.

Papa picked her up.

He held her close to Gracie.

Little Lady snarled.

Uh-oh, thought Brother,

they're not

going to get along.

Little Lady bared her teeth.

But Gracie was not frightened.

She reached out and popped Little Lady
on the nose with her tiny sharp claws.
Little Lady ran away.

"Hmm," said Papa.

"I think they are going to get along fine."

"What about Gracie and Goldie,
our goldfish?" asked Brother.

"I wouldn't worry," said Papa.

"Little Lady loves Goldie.

She'll protect Goldie."

Gracie was now all clean, dry,
and combed.

Her fur was soft and fluffy.

She was very beautiful.

"So I guess we've got a new kitten,"
said Mama.

"Yippee!" cried Brother and Sister.

They took Gracie to the vet

to be checked.

Little Lady went with them.

Her tail was between her legs.

She looked unhappy.

The vet checked Gracie from head to toe.

"She's a fine, healthy kitten," said the vet.

"But I do have a prescription

for Little Lady."

He wrote something on a piece of paper.

Here is what it said:

Prescription—Little Lady might be jealous

for a few days.

So give her at least twenty

extra hugs a day.

Right then and there

Little Lady got her first big hug of the day.

"Mew! Mew!" said Gracie.